Los tres osos

The Three Bears

Querido padre o tutor: Es posible que los libros de esta serie para lectores principiantes les resulten familiares, ya que las versiones originales de los mismos podrían haber formado parte de sus primeras lecturas. Estos textos, cuidadosamente escritos, incluyen palabras de uso frecuente que le proveen al niño la oportunidad de familiarizarse con las más comúnmente usadas en el lenguaje escrito. Estas nuevas versiones han sido actualizadas y las encantadoras ilustraciones son sumamente atractivas para una nueva generación de pequeños lectores.

Primero, léale el cuento al niño, después permita que él lea las palabras con las que esté familiarizado, y pronto podrá leer solito todo el cuento. En cada paso, elogie el esfuerzo del niño para que desarrolle confianza como lector independiente. Hable sobre las ilustraciones y anime al niño a relacionar el cuento con su propia vida.

Al final del cuento, encontrará actividades relacionadas con la lectura que ayudarán a su niño a practicar y fortalecer sus habilidades como lector. Estas actividades, junto con las preguntas de comprensión, se adhieren a los estándares actuales, de manera que la lectura en casa apoyará directamente los objetivos de instrucción en el salón de clase.

Sobre todo, la parte más importante de toda la experiencia de la lectura es ¡divertirse y disfrutarla!

Dear Caregiver: The books in this Beginning-to-Read collection may look somewhat familiar in that the original versions could have been a part of your own early reading experiences. These carefully written texts feature common sight words to provide your child multiple exposures to the words appearing most frequently in written text. These new versions have been updated and the engaging illustrations are highly appealing to a contemporary audience of young readers.

Begin by reading the story to your child, followed by letting him or her read familiar words and soon your child will be able to read the story independently. At each step of the way, be sure to praise your reader's efforts to build his or her confidence as an independent reader. Discuss the pictures and encourage your child to make connections between the story and his or her own life.

At the end of the story, you will find reading activities that will help your child practice and strengthen beginning reading skills. These activities, along with the comprehension questions are aligned to current standards, so reading efforts at home will directly support the instructional goals in the classroom.

Above all, the most important part of the reading experience is to have fun and enjoy it!

Shannon Cannon

Shannon Cannon, Ph.D., Consultora de lectoescritura / Literacy Consultant

Norwood House Press • www.norwoodhousepress.com
Beginning-to-Read ™ is a registered trademark of Norwood House Press.
Illustration and cover design copyright ©2018 by Norwood House Press. All Rights Reserved.

Authorized Bilingual adaptation from the U.S. English language edition, entitled The Three Bears by Margaret Hillert. Copyright © 2017 Pearson Education, Inc. or its affiliates. Bilingual adaptation Copyright © 2018 Pearson Education, Inc. or its affiliates. Translated and adapted with permission. All rights reserved. Pearson and Los tres osos are trademarks, in the US and/or other countries, of Pearson Education, Inc. or its affiliates. This publication is protected by copyright, and prior permission to re-use in any way in any format is required by both Norwood House Press and Pearson Education.   This book is authorized in the United States for use in schools and public libraries.

Designer: Ron Jaffe   •   Editorial Production: Lisa Walsh

LIBRARY OF CONGRESS CATALOGING-IN-PUBLICATION DATA

Names: Hillert, Margaret, author. I Undercuffler, Gary, illustrator. I Del
  Risco, Eida, translator.
Title: Los tres osos = The three bears / por Margaret Hillert ; ilustrado por
  Gary Undercuffler ; traducido por Eida Del Risco.
Other titles: Three bears I Goldilocks and the three bears. English.
Description: Chicago, Illinois : Norwood House Press, [2017] I Summary: "An
  easy to read fairy tale about Goldilocks and the Three Bears and the
  girl's visit to the bears' house. Spanish/English edition includes reading
  activities"-- Provided by publisher.
Identifiers: LCCN 2016057982 (print) I LCCN 2017014223 (ebook) I ISBN
  9781684040643 (eBook) I ISBN 9781599538501 (library edition : alk. paper)
Subjects: I CYAC: Folklore. I Bears--Folklore. I Spanish language
  materials--Bilingual.
Classification: LCC PZ74.1 (ebook) I LCC PZ74.1 .H548 2017 (print) I DDC
  398.2 [E] –dc23
LC record available at https://lccn.loc.gov/2016057982

Hardcover ISBN: 978-1-59953-850-1   Paperback ISBN: 978-1-68404-049-0

302N—072017
Manufactured in the United States of America in North Mankato, Minnesota.

Los tres osos
The Three Bears

Contado por/Retold by Margaret Hillert
Ilustrado por/Illustrated by Gary Undercuffler

NORWOOD HOUSE PRESS

Mira la casa.
Es roja y amarilla.
Es una casita graciosa.

See the house.
It is red and yellow.
It is a funny little house.

Uno, dos, tres.
Uno es el papá.
Uno es la mamá.
Uno es el bebé.

One, two, three.
One is the father.
One is the mother.
One is the baby.

El papá es grande.
El bebé es pequeño.

The father is big.
The baby is little.

Mira trabajar a mamá.
Mamá puede hacer algo.

See Mother work.
Mother can make something.

Nos vamos.
Lejos, lejos, lejos.

Away we go.
Away, away, away.

Puedo jugar.
Mi pelota es azul.
Mira como sube.

I can play.
My ball is blue.
See it go up.

Ay, mira.
Aquí hay una casita.
Una casita graciosa.
Puedo entrar.

Oh, look.
Here is a little house.
A funny little house.
I can go in.

Aquí hay algo.
Rojo, amarillo y azul.
Uno es grande.
Uno es pequeño.

Here is something.
Red, yellow, and blue.
One is big.
One is little.

Quiero algo.
Aquí hay uno para mí.

I want something.
Here is one for me.

Aquí hay algo.
Rojo, amarillo y azul.
Uno es grande.
Uno es pequeño.

Here is something.
Red, yellow, and blue.
One is big.
One is little.

Aquí hay una para mí.

Here is one for me.

Aquí hay algo.
Roja, amarilla y azul.
Una es grande.
Una es pequeña.

Here is something.
Red, yellow, and blue.
One is big.
One is little.

Aquí hay una para mí.

Here is one for me.

Aquí llegamos.
Podemos entrar.

Here we come.
We can go in.

—¡Ay, ay! —dijo el papá.
—¡Vaya, vaya! —dijo la mamá.
—¡Ay, mira! —dijo el bebé—. No hay nada aquí.

Father said, "Oh, oh!"
Mother said, "Oh, my!"
Baby said, "Oh, look! It is not here."

—¡Ay, ay! —dijo el papá.
—¡Vaya, vaya! —dijo la mamá.
—¡Ay, mira! —dijo el bebé—. Se cayó.

Father said, "Oh, oh!"
Mother said, "Oh, my!"
Baby said, "Oh, look! It is down."

—¡Ay, ay! —dijo el papá.
—¡Vaya, vaya! —dijo la mamá.
—¡Ay, mira! —dijo el bebé—. Veo algo.

Father said, "Oh, oh!"
Mother said, "Oh, my!"
Baby said, "Oh, look! I see something."

¡Ayuda! ¡Ayuda!
Puedo saltar.
Puedo correr.

Help, help!
I can jump down.
I can run.

Ay, mamá, mamá.
¡Aquí estoy!

Oh, Mother, Mother.
Here I am!

27

READING REINFORCEMENT

Foundational Skills

In addition to reading the numerous high-frequency words in the text, this book also supports the development of foundational skills.

Phonological Awareness: The /s/ sound

Oddity Task: Say the /s/ sound for your child. Say the following words aloud. Ask your child to say the word that does not end with the /s/ sound in the following word groups:

bus, yes, yet	gas, gab, kiss	cab, bats, cabs	miss, mess, mix
us, play, plus	this, less, fast	set, loss, toss	past, pass, pats

Phonics: The letter Ss

1. Demonstrate how to form the letters **S** and **s** for your child.
2. Have your child practice writing **S** and **s** at least three times each.
3. Ask your child to point to the words in the book that start with the letter **s**.
4. Write down the following words and ask your child to circle the letter **s** in each word:

see	sit	is	Sam	say	was
saw	bears	sat	kiss	something	she
basket	pass	star	said	house	sun

Fluency: Shared Reading

1. Reread the story to your child at least two more times while your child tracks the print by running a finger under the words as they are read. Ask your child to read the words he or she knows with you.
2. Reread the story taking turns, alternating readers between sentences or pages.

Language

The concepts, illustrations, and text help children develop language both explicitly and implicitly.

Vocabulary: Number Words

1. Explain to your child that numbers can be written as words or numerals.
2. Write the following words on separate pieces of paper:

| zero | one | two | three | four | five |
| six | seven | eight | nine | ten | |

3. Read each word to your child and ask your child to repeat it.
4. Mix the words up. Point to a word and ask your child to read it. Provide clues if your child needs them.
5. Hold up any number of fingers from zero to ten and ask your child to point to the correct word that represents that number.
6. Write the numbers 0–10 on separate pieces of paper and ask your child to match the numerals with the number words.
7. When your child has mastered these first numbers, you may wish to repeat the activity again for numbers eleven to twenty.

Reading Literature and Informational Text

To support comprehension, ask your child the following questions. The answers either come directly from the text or require inferences and discussion.

Key Ideas and Detail

- Ask your child to retell the sequence of events in the story.
- Who are the members of the bear family?

Craft and Structure

- Is this a book that tells a story or one that gives information? How do you know?
- How do you think the bears felt when they came home?

Integration of Knowledge and Ideas

- Why do you think the girl was sleeping when the bears came home?
- Who are the people in your family?

ACERCA DE LA AUTORA

Margaret Hillert ha ayudado a millones de niños de todo el mundo a aprender a leer independientemente. Fue maestra de primer grado por 34 años y durante esa época empezó a escribir libros con los que sus estudiantes pudieran ganar confianza en la lectura y pudieran, al mismo tiempo, disfrutarla. Ha escrito más de 100 libros para niños que comienzan a leer. De niña, disfrutaba escribiendo poesía y, de adulta, continuó su escritura poética tanto para niños como para adultos.

Photograph by Glenna Washburn

ABOUT THE AUTHOR

Margaret Hillert has helped millions of children all over the world learn to read independently. She was a first grade teacher for 34 years and during that time started writing books that her students could both gain confidence in reading and enjoy. She wrote well over 100 books for children just learning to read. As a child, she enjoyed writing poetry and continued her poetic writings as an adult for both children and adults.

ACERCA DEL ILUSTRADOR

Durante treinta años, Gary Undercuffler ha ilustrado una gran variedad de libros para niños, libros de texto y lecturas escolares. Enseña ilustración, dibujo y computación gráfica en una universidad local. Siempre encuentra tiempo para dibujar en sus cuadernos de bocetos, hacer dibujos de figuras y, de cuando en cuando, tocar la guitarra. Gary vive feliz con su esposa Diana, en una acogedora casita en Pensilvania, casi tan bonita con la cabaña de los tres osos. www.garyundercuffler.com

ABOUT THE ILLUSTRATOR

Over the past thirty years, Gary Undercuffler has illustrated a wide variety of children's books, textbooks, and school readers. He teaches illustration, drawing, and computer graphics at a local area college. He also finds time to draw in his sketchbooks, do figure drawings, and occasionally play guitar. Gary lives happily with his wife, Diana, in a cozy home in Pennsylvania—almost as cute as The Three Bears' cottage. www.garyundercuffler.com